PRAISE FOR
The Barracks Thief

"There is a real power in this slim novel . . ."
—Anne Tyler

"Tobias Wolff has somehow gotten his hands on our shared secrets, and he's out to tell everything he knows."
—Raymond Carver

THE BARRACKS THIEF

ALSO BY TOBIAS WOLFF

In the Garden of the North American Martyrs

THE
BARRACKS
THIEF

TOBIAS WOLFF

An Imprint of HarperCollinsPublishers

HarperCollins books may be purchased for educational, business, or sales promotional use. For information please write: Special Markets Department, HarperCollins Publishers Inc., 10 East 53rd Street, New York, NY 10022.

Library of Congress Cataloging-in-publication Data
  Wolff, Tobias, 1945– The barracks thief.
    1. Vietnamese Conflict, 1961–1975—Fiction. I. Title.
  PS3573.0558B3   1983
  813'.54   83-16422
  ISBN 0-88001-049-5 (PBK.)

  11 12 13 BV/RRD 10 9 8

For Laudie

Grateful acknowledgment is made to *Antaeus* and to *Granta* (England) where the contents of this book first appeared.

My thanks to the Arizona Council on the Arts and Humanities for their generous support. — TW

THE BARRACKS THIEF

1

When his boys were young, Guy Bishop formed the habit of stopping in their room each night on his way to bed. He would look down at them where they slept, and then he would sit in the rocking chair and listen to them breathe. He was a man who had always gone from one thing to another, place to place, job to job, and, even since his marriage, woman to woman. But when he sat in the dark between his two sleeping sons he felt no wish to move.

Sometimes, because it seemed unnatural, this peace he felt gave him fears. The worst fear he had was that by loving his children so much he was somehow endangering them, putting them in harm's way. At times he knew for a certainty that some evil was about to overtake them. As the boys grew older he had this fear less often, but it still came upon him from time to time. Then he tried to imagine what form the evil might take, from which direction it might come. When he had these thoughts Guy Bishop would close his eyes, give his head a little shake, and turn his mind to some more pleasant subject.

He was seeing a woman off and on. They had

good times together and that was all either of them wanted, at least in the beginning. Then they began to feel miserable when they were away from each other. They agreed to break it off, but couldn't. There were nights when Guy Bishop woke up weeping. At one point he considered killing himself, but the woman made him promise not to. When he couldn't hold out any longer he left his family and went to live with her.

This was in October. Keith, the younger of the boys, had just begun his freshman year in high school. Philip was a junior. Guy Bishop thought that they were old enough to accept this change and even to grow stronger from it, more realistic and adaptable. Most of the worry he felt was for his wife. He knew that the break-up of their marriage was going to cause her terrible suffering, and he did what he could to arrange things so that, except for his leaving, her life would not be disrupted. He signed the house over to her and each month he sent her most of his salary, holding back only what he needed to live on.

Philip did learn to get along without his father, mainly by despising him. His mother held up, too, better than Guy Bishop had expected. She caved in every couple of weeks or so, but most of the time she was cheerful in a determined way. Only Keith lost heart. He could not stop grieving. He cried easily, sometimes for no apparent reason. The two boys had been close; now, even in the act of comforting Keith, Philip looked at him from a distance. There was only a year and a half between them but it began to seem like five or six. One night, coming in from a party, he shook Keith awake with the idea of having a good talk, but after Keith woke up Philip went on shaking him and didn't say a word. One of the cats had been sleeping with Keith. She arched her back, stared wide-eyed at Philip, and jumped to the floor.

"You've got to do your part," Philip said.

Keith just looked at him.

"Damn you," Philip said. He pushed Keith back against the pillow. "Cry," he said. "Go ahead, cry." He really did hope that Keith would cry, because he wanted to hold him. But Keith shook his head. He turned his face to the wall. After that Keith kept his feelings to himself.

In February Guy Bishop lost his job at Boeing. He told everyone that the company was laying people off, but the opposite was true. This was 1965. President Johnson had turned the bombers loose on North Vietnam and Boeing had orders for more planes than they could build. They were bringing people in from all over, men from Lockheed and Convair, boys fresh out of college. It seemed that anyone could work at Boeing but Guy Bishop. Philip's mother called the wives of men who might know what the trouble was, but either they hadn't heard or they weren't saying.

Guy Bishop found another job but he didn't stay with it, and just before school let out Philip's mother put the house up for sale. She gave away all but one of her five cats and took a job as cashier in a movie theater downtown. It was the same work she'd been doing when Guy Bishop met her in 1945. The house sold within a month. A retired Coast Guard captain bought it. He drove by the house nearly every day with his wife and sometimes they parked in front with the engine running.

Philip's mother took an apartment in West Seattle. Philip worked as a camp counselor that summer, and while he was away she and Keith moved again, to Ballard. In the fall both boys enrolled at Ballard High. It was a big school, much bigger than the one where they'd gone before, and it was hard to meet people. Philip kept in touch with his old friends, but now that they weren't in school together they found little to talk about. When he went to parties with them he usually ended up sitting by himself in the living room, watching television or talking to some kid's parents while everyone else slow-danced in the rec room downstairs.

After one of these parties Philip and the boy who'd brought him sat in the boy's car and passed a paper cup full of vodka back and forth and talked about things they used to do. At some point in their conversation Philip realized that they weren't friends anymore. He felt restless and got out of the car. He stood there, looking at the darkened house across the street. He wanted to do something. He wished he was drunk.

"I've got to go," the other boy said. "My dad wants me in early tonight."

"Just a minute," Philip said. He picked up a rock, hefted it, then threw it at the house. A window broke. "One down," Philip said. He picked up another rock.

"Jesus," the other boy said. "What are you doing?"

"Breaking windows," Philip said. At that moment a light came on upstairs. He threw the rock but it missed and banged against the side of the house.

"I'm getting out of here," the other boy said. He started the car and Philip got back inside. He began to laugh as they drove away, though he knew there was nothing funny about what he'd done. The other boy stared straight ahead and said nothing. Philip could see that he was disgusted. "Wait a minute," Philip said, grabbing the sleeve of the Nehru jacket the other boy had on. "I don't believe it. Where did you get the Nehru jacket?" When the other boy didn't answer Philip said, "Don't tell me—it's your dad's. That's why your dad wants you home early. He likes to know where his Nehru jacket is."

When they got to Philip's apartment building

they sat for a moment without talking. Finally Philip said, "I'm sorry," and put out his hand. But the other boy looked away.

Philip got out of the car. "I'll give you a call," he said, and when he got no response he added: "I was just kidding about the Nehru jacket. It must have looked really great about twenty years ago."

Philip had always wanted to go to Reed College, but by the time he finished high school that year his grades were so bad he was lucky to graduate at all. Reed sent him a form rejection letter and so did the University of Washington, his second choice. He went to work as a busboy in a motel restaurant and tried to stay out of the apartment. Keith was always there, playing records or just lying around, his sadness plain to see though he had begun to affect a breezy manner of speech. Philip suspected that he was stoned a lot of the time, but he didn't know what to do about it, or if he should do anything at all. Though he felt sorry for Keith, Philip was beginning to dislike him. He wanted to avoid anything that might cause trouble between them and add to the dislike he felt. Besides, he had a smoke now and then himself. It made him feel interesting—witty, sensitive, perceptive.

Sometimes the owner of the theater where she worked gave Philip's mother a ride home. One night, coming home late himself, he saw them kissing in the owner's car. Philip turned around and went back up the street. The next day he refused to speak to her, and refused to tell her why, though he knew he was being theatrical and unfair. Finally it drove her to tears. As he sat reading Philip heard her cry out in the kitchen. He jumped up, thinking she must have burned herself. He found her leaning on the sink, her face in her hands. What had happened to them? Where were they? Where was her home, her cats, her garden? Where was the regard of her neighbors, the love of her family? Everything was gone.

Philip did his best to calm her. It wasn't easy, but after a time she agreed to go for a walk with him, and managed to collect herself. Philip knew he had been in the wrong. He told his mother that he was sorry, and that his moodiness had had nothing to do with her — he was just a little on edge. She squeezed his arm. This won't go on forever, Philip thought. In silence, they continued to walk the circular path around the small park. It was August and still warm, but the benches were empty. Now and then a pigeon landed with a rush of wings, looked around, and flew away again.

Their parish priest from the old neighborhood had friends among the local Jesuits. He succeeded in getting Philip a probationary acceptance to Seattle University. It was a good school, but Philip wanted to get away from home. In September he moved to Bremerton and enrolled at the junior college there. During the day he tried to keep awake in his classes and at night he worked at the Navy Yard, doing inventory in warehouses and dodging forklifts driven by incompetents.

Philip didn't get to know many people in Bremerton, but sometimes when he got off work at midnight he went drinking with a few of the Marine guards. Bremerton was a soft berth for them after a year in Vietnam. They'd been in the fighting, and some of them had been wounded. They were all a little crazy. Philip didn't understand their jokes, and if he laughed anyway they gave him mean looks. They talked about "asshole civilians" as if he weren't there.

The Marines tolerated Philip because he had a car, an old Pontiac he'd bought for fifty dollars at a police auction. He ferried them to different bars and sometimes to parties, then back to the Yard through misty wet streets, trying to keep his eyes open while they laughed and yelled out the window and threw beer on each other. If one of them got into a fight all the others piled in immediately, no questions asked. Philip was often amazed at their brutishness, but there were times, after he'd let them off and watched them go through the gate together, when he envied them.

At Christmas Philip's mother asked him to talk to Keith. Keith was doing badly in school, and just before vacation one of his teachers had caught him smoking a joint in a broom closet. He'd been alone, which seemed grotesque to Philip. When he thought of Keith standing in the dark surrounded by brooms and cleanser and rolls of toilet paper, puffing away all by himself, he felt disgusted. Only by going down to the school and pleading with the principal, "groveling," as she put it, had Philip's mother been able to dissuade him from reporting Keith to the police. As it was, he'd been suspended for two weeks.

"I'll talk to him," Philip said, "but it won't do any good."

"It might," she said. "He looks up to you. Remember the way he used to follow you around?"

They were sitting in the living room. Philip's mother was smoking and had her feet on the coffee table. Her toenails were painted red. She caught Philip staring at them and looked down at her drink.

"My life isn't going anywhere," Philip said. He got up and walked over to the window. "I'm going to enlist," he said. This was an idea he'd had for some time now, but hearing himself put it in words surprised him and gave him a faint sensation of fear.

His mother sat forward. "Enlist? Why would you want to enlist?"

"In case you haven't heard," Philip said, "there's

a war on." That sounded false to him and he could see it sounded false to his mother as well. "It's just something I want to do," he said. He shrugged.

His mother put her glass down. "When?"

"Pretty soon."

"Give me a year," she said. She stood and came over to Philip. "Give me six months, anyway. Try to understand. This thing with Keith has got me coming and going."

"Keith," Philip said. He shook his head. Finally he agreed to wait the six months.

They spent Christmas day in the apartment. Philip gave Keith a puzzle that he worked on all afternoon and never came close to solving, though it looked simple enough to Philip. They had dinner in a restaurant and after they got back Keith went at the puzzle again, still with no success. Philip wanted to help, but whenever he offered a suggestion Keith went on as if he hadn't heard. Philip watched him, impatiently at first, then thoughtfully; he wondered what it was in Keith that found satisfaction in losing. If he went on the way he was, losing would become a habit, and he would never be able to pull his weight.

They had their talk but it went badly, as Philip knew it would. Though he tried to be gentle, he ended up calling Keith a coward. Keith laughed and made sarcastic remarks about Philip going into the service. He had suddenly decided that he was against the war. Philip pointed out that it had taken Keith seven tries to pass his driver's license examination, and said that anyone who had that much trouble driving a car, or solving a simple puzzle, had no right to an opinion on any subject.

"That's it," Philip told his mother afterwards. "Never again."

A few nights later Philip came back from a movie and found his mother in tears and Keith trying to soothe her, though it was obvious that he was close to the breaking point himself. Oh, hell, Philip thought, but it wasn't what he had assumed. They weren't just feeling sorry for themselves. Philip's father had come by and when they refused to open the door for him he had tried to break in. He'd made a scene, yelling at them and ramming the door with his shoulder.

Philip left Keith with his mother and drove out to his father's place in Bellevue, an efficiency apartment near the lake. Guy Bishop had moved to Bellevue a few months earlier when the woman he'd been living with went to Sarasota to visit her family, and decided to stay there.

He still had his windbreaker on when he opened the door. "Philip," he said. "Come in." Philip shook his head. "Please, son," his father said, "come in."

They sat at a counter that divided the kitchen from the rest of the room. There were several pairs of gleaming shoes lined up along the wall, and the air smelled of shoe polish. On the coffee table there was a family portrait taken at Mount Rushmore in 1963. Keith and Philip were in the middle, grinning because the photographer, a Canadian, had just said "aboot" for "about." The four presidents, eyes blank, seemed to be looking down at them. Next to the picture a stack of magazines had been arranged in a fan, so that a strip of each cover was visible.

Philip told his father to stay away from the apartment. That was where the family lived, Philip said, and Guy Bishop wasn't part of the family.

Suddenly his father reached out and put his hand on Philip's cheek. Philip stared down at the counter. A moment later his father took his hand away. Of course, he said. He would call first thing in the morning and apologize.

"Forget the apology," Philip said. "Just leave her alone, period."

"It's not that simple," his father said. "She called me first."

"What do you mean, she called you first?"

"She asked me to come over," he said. "When I got there she wouldn't let me in. Which is no excuse for acting the way I did." He folded his hands and looked down at them.

"I don't believe you," Philip said.

His father shrugged. A moment later he looked over at Philip and smiled. "I've got something for you. It was meant to be a graduation present, but I didn't have a chance to give it to you then." He went over to the closet and pulled out a suitcase. "Come on," he said.

Philip followed him out of the room and down the steps into the parking lot. It had rained. The pavement shone under the lights, and the cars gleamed. Philip's father bent down and unzipped the suitcase. It was full of what looked like silver pipes. He lifted them out all at once, and Philip saw that they were connected. His father arranged them, tightening wing-nuts here and there, until finally a frame took shape with prongs at each end. He got two wheels from the suitcase and fastened them between the prongs. Then he bolted a leather seat to the top of the frame. It was a bicycle, a folding bicycle. He put down the kick-stand and stepped back.

"Voila," he said.

They looked at it.

"It works," he said. He put up the kick-stand and straddled it, searching with his feet for the pedals. He pushed himself around the parking lot, bumping into cars, wobbling badly. With its little wheels and elevated seat the bicycle looked like the kind bears ride in circuses. The chrome frame glittered. The spokes caught the light as they went around and around.

"You'll never be without transportation," Philip's father said. "You can keep it in the trunk of your car. Then, if something breaks down or you run out of gas, you won't be forced to hitchhike." He almost fell taking a turn but managed to right himself. "Or say you go to Europe. What better way," he said, and then the bicycle caught the fender of a car and he pitched over the handlebars. He fell heavily. The bicycle came down with him and he lay there, all tangled up in it.

"My God," he said. "Give me a hand, son." When Philip didn't come to him he said, "I can't move. Give me a hand."

Philip turned and walked toward his car.

The next morning Philip got up early and took a bus downtown. The Marine recruiting office was closed. He wandered around, and when it still hadn't opened two hours later he walked up the street and enlisted in the Army. That night, when he knew his mother would be at work, he called home from Fort Lewis. At first Keith thought he was joking. Then the idea took hold. "You're really in the Army," he said. "What a trip. Jesus. Well, good luck. I mean that."

Philip could tell he was serious. It touched him, and he did something he came to regret. He gave Keith his car.

2

Five months later Keith disappeared. I was in jump school at Fort Benning when it happened, at the tail end of a training course that proved harder than anything I had ever done.

When I got the message to call home we had just come back from our third of five parachute jumps. We'd been dropped after a heavy rain and landed in mud to our ankles, struggling against a wind that pulled us down and dragged us through a mess of other men, scrub pine, tangled silk and rope. I was still spitting out mud when we got back to camp.

My mother told me that Keith had been gone for three days. He had left no message, not even a good-bye. The police had a description of the car and they'd talked to his friends, but so far they seemed no closer to finding him. We agreed that he had probably gone to San Francisco.

"No doubt about it," I said. "That's where all the losers are going now."

"Don't take that tone," she said. "It breaks my heart to hear you talk like that. Is that what you're learning in the Army?"

It had started to rain again. I was using an unsheltered pay phone near the orderly room, and the rain began to melt the caked mud on my uniform. Brown streams of it ran off my boots. "What do you want me to do?" I asked.

"I want you to go to San Francisco and look for Keith."

I couldn't help laughing. "Now how am I supposed to do that? This is Georgia, remember?"

"I've talked to a man at the Red Cross," she said. "You could get an emergency leave. They'll even lend you money."

"That's ridiculous," I said, though I realized what she was saying was true. I could go on leave. But I didn't want to. It would mean missing the last two jumps, dropping out of the course. If I came back I would have to start all over again. I doubted I had the courage to do that; jump school was no day at the beach and I'd only made it this far out of ignorance of what lay ahead. I wanted those wings. I wanted them more than anything.

And if I did go, where would I look? Who would help me in San Francisco, me with my head shaved to the bone in a city full of freaks?

"You have to," she said. "He's your brother."

"I'm sorry," I told her. "It's just not possible."

"But he's so young. What is happening to us? Will somebody please tell me what is happening to us?"

I said that the police would find Keith, that he'd

be glad to get home, that a taste of the real world would give him a new angle on things. I didn't believe what I was saying, but it calmed her down. Finally she let me go.

On our last jump, a night jump in full field equipment, a man was killed. His main chute didn't open. I heard him yell going down but it only lasted a moment and I paid no attention. Some clown was always yelling. It ended and there was no sound save the rhythmic creaking of my shoulder straps. I felt the air move past my face. The full moon lit up the silk above me, above the hundred other men falling in silence overhead and below and all around me. It seemed that every one of us fell under his own moon. Then a tree stabbed up to my right and I braced and hit the ground rolling.

The dead man was carried to the side of the road and left there for the ambulance. They didn't bother to cover him up. They wanted us to take a good look, and remember him, because he had screwed up. He had forgotten to pull his reserve parachute. As our truck went past him a sergeant said, "There's just two kinds of men in this business—the quick and the dead."

The fellow across from me laughed. So did several others. I didn't laugh, but I felt the impulse. The man lying by the road had been alive an hour ago, and now he was dead. Why did that make me want to smile? It seemed wrong. Someone was passing around a number. I took a hit and gave it to the man next to me. "All right!" he said. "Airborne!"

Two black guys started a jump song. I leaned back and looked up at the stars and after a while I joined in the song the others were singing.

3

After jump school I was sent to the 82nd Airborne Division at Fort Bragg. Most of the men in my company had served together in Vietnam. Like the Marines I'd known in Bremerton, they had no use for outsiders. I was an outsider to them. So were the other new men, Lewis and Hubbard. The three of us didn't exist for the rest of the company. For days at a time nobody spoke to me except to give me orders. Because we were the newest and lowest in rank we got picked to pull guard duty on the Fourth of July while everyone else scattered to Myrtle Beach and the air-conditioned bars in Fayetteville.

That's where I'd wanted to spend the Fourth, in a bar. There was one place in particular I liked. Smitty's. They had a go-go dancer at Smitty's who chewed gum while she danced. Prostitutes, Fayettecong we called them, gathered in the booths with pitchers of beer between them. Car salesmen from the lots down the street sat around figuring out ways to unload monster Bonnevilles on buck privates who made seventy-eight dollars a month before taxes. The bartender knew my name.

The last way I wanted to spend my Fourth was pulling guard with Lewis and Hubbard. We had arrived on the same day and avoided each other ever since. I could see that they were as lonely as I was, but we kept our distance; if we banded together we would always be new.

So when I saw the duty roster and found myself lumped together with them it made me bitter. Lewis and Hubbard were bitter, too. I could feel it in the way they looked at me when I joined them outside the orderly room. They didn't greet me, and while we waited for the duty officer they stared off in different directions. It was late afternoon but still steaming. The straight lines of the camp—files of barracks, flagpoles, even the white-washed rocks arranged in rows—wavered in the heat. Locusts sawed away in frantic bursts.

Lewis, gaunt and red-faced, began to whistle. Then he stopped. Our uniforms darkened with sweat. The oil on our rifles stank. Our faces glistened. The silence between us grew intense and I was glad when the first sergeant came up and began to shout at us.

He told us that we were little girls, piglets, warts. We were toads. We didn't belong in his army. He lined us up and inspected us. He said that we should be court-martialed for our ugliness and stupidity. Then he drove us to an ammunition dump in the middle of a pine forest thirty miles from the post and made us stand with our rifles over our heads while he gave us our orders and filled our clips with live rounds. We were to patrol the perimeter of the ammunition dump until he relieved us. He didn't say when that would be. If anyone so much as touched the fence we should shoot to kill. *Shoot to kill*, he repeated. No yakking. No grabass. If we screwed up he would personally bring grief upon us. "I know everything," he said, and he ordered us to run around the compound with our rifles still over our heads. When we got back he was gone, along with the three men whose places we had taken.

Lewis had the first shift. Hubbard and I sat in the shade of an old warehouse weathered down to bare gray boards with patches of green paint curling off. It had no windows. On the loading ramp where we sat two sliding doors were padlocked together and plastered with prohibitions, *No Smoking* and so on, with a few strange ones thrown in, like *No Hobnailed Boots*.

There were five other buildings, all in bad repair. Weeds grew between the buildings and alongside the chain-link fence. In places the weeds were waist-high. I don't know what kind of ammunition was inside the buildings.

Hubbard and I put our ponchos under our heads and tried to sleep. But we couldn't lie still. Gnats crawled up our noses. Mosquitoes hung in clouds around our heads. The air smelled like turpentine from the resin oozing out of the trees.

"I wish I was home," Hubbard said.

"Me too," I said. There didn't seem to be much point in ignoring Hubbard out here, where nobody could see me do it. But the word "home" meant nothing anymore. My father was in Southern California, looking for work. Keith was still missing. The last time I'd spoken to her my mother's voice had been cold, as if I were somehow to blame.

"If I was home," Hubbard said, "I'd be out at the drags with Vogel and Kirk. Don't ask me what I'm doing here because I sure don't know." He took off his helmet and wiped his face with his sleeve. He had a soft, square face with a little roll of flesh under his chin. It was the face he'd have for the rest of his life. "Look," he said. He took out his wallet and showed me a picture of a '49 Mercury.

"Nice," I said.

"It isn't mine." Hubbard looked at the picture and then put it away. "I was going to buy it before Uncle got me. I wouldn't race it, though. I'd take it out to the track and sit on the hood with Vogel and Kirk and drink beer."

Hubbard went on talking about Vogel and Kirk. Then he stopped and shook his head. "How about you?" he asked. "What would you be doing if you were home?"

"If I were home," I said, remembering us all together, "we would drive up to the fair at Mount Vernon. Then we'd have dinner at my grandfather's place—he has this big barbecue every year—and afterwards we'd stay in a motel with a swimming pool. My brother and I would swim all night and watch the fireworks from the water."

We had not been to Mount Vernon since my grandfather died when I was fourteen, so the memory was an old one. But it didn't feel old. It felt fresh and true, the starry night, the soft voices from the open doorways around the pool, the water so warm you forgot about it, forgot your own skin. Shaking hands with Keith underwater and looking up from the bottom of the pool at the rockets flaring overhead, the wrinkled surface of the water all ashimmer with their light. My father on the balcony above, leaning over the rail, calling down to us. That's enough, boys. Come in. It's late.

"You like it, don't you?" Hubbard asked.

"Like what?"

"All this stuff. Marching everywhere. Carrying a rifle. The Army."

"Come off it," I said. I shook my head.

"It's true," he said. "I can tell."

I shook my head again but made no further denials. Hubbard's admission that the car in the picture wasn't his had put me in an honest mood. And I was flattered that he had taken the trouble to come to a conclusion about me. Even this one. "The Army has its good points," I said.

"Name me one." Hubbard leaned against the ramp. He closed his eyes. I could hear Lewis whistling as he walked along the fence.

I couldn't explain why I liked the Army because I didn't understand the reason myself. "Travel," I said. "You can go all over the world."

Hubbard opened his eyes. "You know where I've been to? South Carolina, Georgia, and North Carolina. All I've seen is a lot of hicks. And when they do send us overseas it will just be to kill slopes. You know the first sergeant? They say he killed over twenty of them. I could never do that. I shot a squirrel once and cried all night."

We talked some more and Hubbard told me that he hadn't been drafted, as I'd assumed. Like me, he had enlisted. He said that the Army had tricked him. They'd sent a recruiter to his high school just before graduation to talk to the boys in Hubbard's class. The recruiter got them together in the gym and ran movies of soldiers being massaged by girls in Korea, and drinking beer in Germany out of steins. Then he visited the boys in their homes and showed each of them why the Army was the right choice. He told Hubbard that anyone who could drive a tractor automatically got to drive a tank, which turned out not to be true. Hubbard hadn't even set foot in a tank, not once. "Of course he didn't mention Vietnam," Hubbard said.

When I asked Hubbard what he was doing in the Airborne he shrugged. "I thought it might be interesting," he said. "I should have known better. Just more of the same. People running around yelling their heads off."

He waved his hand through a swarm of mosquitoes overhead. "We'll be getting orders pretty soon," he said. "Are you scared?"

I nodded. "A little. I don't think about it much."

"I think about it all the time. I just hope I don't get killed. They can shoot my dick off as long as they don't kill me."

I didn't know what to say. The sound of Lewis's whistling grew louder.

"Nuts," Hubbard said. "I don't know what he's so cheerful about."

Lewis came around the corner and climbed the ramp. "Shift's up," he said. "Best watch how you go along that fence. There's nettles poking through everyplace." He held out his hand for us to see. It was swollen and red. He leaned his rifle against the warehouse and began to unlace his boots.

"I'm allergic to nettles," Hubbard said. "I could die out there." He stood and put on his helmet.

"Wish me luck. If I don't make it back tell Laura I love her."

Lewis watched Hubbard go, then turned to me. "I never saw so many bugs in my life," he said. "Wish I was at the beach. You ever been to Nag's Head? Those girls up there just go and go."

"Never been there," I said.

"I had one of those girls almost tore my back off," Lewis said. "Still got the marks." He leaned towards me and for a moment there I thought he was going to take his shirt off and show me his back as he'd shown me his hand.

"Ever been to Kentucky?" he asked.

I shook my head.

"That's where I'm from. Lawton. It's a dry town but I've been drinking since I was thirteen. Year after that I started on intercourse. Now it's got to where I can't go to sleep anymore unless I ate pussy."

"I'm from Washington," I said. "The state."

Lewis took off his helmet. He had close-cropped hair, red like his face. He could have worn it longer if he'd wanted, now that we were out of training. But he chose to wear it that way. It was his style.

He studied me. "You never been to Lawton," he said. "You ought to go. You won't want to leave and that's a guarantee." He took off one of his socks and started doing something to his foot. It seemed to require all his concentration. He sucked in his long cheeks and stuck the tip of his tongue out of the side of his mouth. "There," he said and wiggled his toes. "I guess you know about what happened the other day," he said. "It wasn't the way you probably heard."

I didn't know what Lewis was talking about, but he gave me no chance to say so.

"I just didn't have the rope fixed right," he said. "I wasn't afraid. You ought to see me go off the high dive back home. I wanted to straighten out the rope was all."

Now I understood. Our company had practiced rappelling the week before off a fifty-foot cliff and someone had refused the descent. I'd heard the first sergeant raising hell but I was at the base of the cliff and couldn't make out what he was saying or see who he was yelling at.

"He called me Tinkerbell," Lewis said.

"He calls everybody that," I said. He did, too. Tinkerbell and Sweety Pie.

"You go ask around home," Lewis told me. "Just talk to those girls back there. They'll tell you if I'm a Tinkerbell."

"He didn't mean anything."

"I know what he meant," Lewis said, and gave me a fierce look. Then he put his sock back on and stared at it. "What's the matter with these fellows here, anyway? Pretty stuck on themselves if you ask me."

"I guess so," I said. "Look, don't mind me. I'm

going to get some sleep before my shift." I closed my eyes. I hoped that Lewis would be quiet. He was starting to get on my nerves. It wasn't just his loud voice or the things he said. He seemed to want something from me.

"There's not one of these fellows would last a day in Lawton," he said. "We've got a guard in the bank that bit a man's tongue out of his head."

I opened my eyes. Lewis was watching me. "It's just because we're new," I said. "They'll be friendlier when we've been around for a while. Now if you don't mind I'm going to catch some sleep."

"What burns me," Lewis said, "is how you meet one of them in the PX or downtown somewhere and they look past you like they never saw you."

Off in the distance a siren wailed. The sound was weak, only a pulse in the air, but Lewis cocked his head at it. He squinted. When the siren stopped Lewis held his listening attitude for a moment, then gave a little shake. "I'm just as good as them," he said. "Look here. You got family?"

I nodded.

"I'm the only one left," Lewis said. "It was me and my dad, but now he's gone too. Heart attack." He shrugged. "That's all right. I get along just fine."

Another siren went off, right in my ear it seemed. The sound made me wince. Then everything went quiet. Lewis's eyes were pink.

Hubbard came around the side of the building

and started up the ramp. I was glad to see him. He waved and I waved back. He gave me an odd stare then and I realized he'd only been flapping mosquitoes out of his face.

"There's a man out by the gate who wants to talk to us," he said.

Lewis started lacing up his boots. "Officer?"

Hubbard shook his head. "Civilian."

"What does he want?" I asked, but Hubbard had already turned away. I followed him and Lewis came after me, muttering to himself and trying to tie his boots.

There was a car parked in the turn-around outside the gate. It had a decal on the door and a red blinker flashing on top, dim in the gray light of early evening. A man was sitting in the front seat. Another man leaned against the fence. He was tall and stooped. He wiped at his face with a red bandana which he put in his back pocket when he saw us coming.

"Okay, mister," Hubbard said, "we're all here."

"Bet you'd rather be someplace else, too." He smiled at us. "Terrible way to spend the holiday."

None of us said anything.

The man stopped smiling. "We have a fire," he said. He pointed to the east, at a black cloud above the trees. "It's an annual event," the man said. "A couple of kids blew up a pipe full of matches. Almost took their hands off." He turned his head and barked twice. He might have been laughing or he might have been coughing.

"So what?" Lewis said.

The man looked at him, then at me. I noticed for the first time that his eyes were blinking steadily. "This isn't the best place to be," he said.

I knew what he meant—the dry weeds, the warped ramshackle buildings, the ammunition inside. "That fire's a mile off at least," I said. "Can't you put it out?"

"I think we can," he said. He tugged at his pants. It must have been a habit. They were already high on his waist, held there by leather suspenders. "The problem is," he said, "if you catch one spark in there that's all she wrote."

Hubbard and I looked at each other.

The man leaned against the fence. "You boys just come with us and I'll see that someone takes you back to Bragg."

"That's a good way to get dead," said Lewis. He cocked his rifle. The bolt slid forward with a sharp, heavy smack, a sound I'd heard thousands of times since joining the Army but never so distinctly. It changed everything. Everything became vivid, interesting.

The man froze. His eyes stopped their endless blinking.

"You heard me," Lewis said. "Let loose of that fence or you're dog meat."

The man stepped back. He stood with his arms at his sides and watched Lewis. I could hear the breath pass in and out of his mouth. A few minutes earlier I had been glad to see him. He was worried about me. He didn't want me to get blown up and that spoke well of him. But when I looked at him now, without weapon, without uniform, without anyone to back him up, I felt hard and cold. Nobody had the right to be that helpless.

None of us spoke. Finally the man turned and went back to the car.

"Godalmighty," Hubbard said. He turned to Lewis. "Why did you do that?"

"He touched the fence," Lewis said.

"You're crazy," Hubbard said. "You're really crazy."

"Maybe I am and maybe I'm not."

"You are," Hubbard said. "Take my word for it. Crazy hick."

"You calling me a hick?" Lewis said.

Out in the car I could see the two men talking. The one Lewis had scared off kept shaking his head.

"Tell me something, hick," Hubbard said. "Tell me what we're supposed to do if this place goes up."

"That's no concern of mine," Lewis said.

"Jesus," Hubbard said. He looked at me, appealing for help. I disappointed him. "What are you grinning at?" he said.

"Nothing," I said. But I might just as well have

said "Everything." I liked this situation. It was interesting. It had a last-stand quality about it. But I didn't really believe that anything would happen, not to me. Getting hurt was just a choice some people made, like bad luck, or growing old.

"I don't believe this," Hubbard said.

"If you don't like it here," Lewis said, "you can go somewheres else. Won't nobody stop you."

Hubbard stared at the hand Lewis was shaking at him. It was beet-red and so bloated that you couldn't see his knuckles anymore. It looked like an enormous baby's hand, even to the crease around the wrist. "Godalmighty," Hubbard said. "Those must have been some killer nettles you ran into. With plants like that I don't know what they need us for."

"Look," I said. "We've got a visitor."

The other man had gotten out of the car and was walking up to the fence. He smiled as he came toward us. "Hello there," he said. He took off his sunglasses as if to show us he had nothing to hide. His face was dark with soot. "I'm Deputy Chief Ellingboe," he said. He held up a card. When we didn't look at it he put it back in his shirt pocket. He glanced over at the man sitting in the car. "You certainly gave old Charlie there something to talk about," he said.

"Old Charlie about got his ears peeled," Lewis said.

"There's no call for that talk," the man said. He

came up to the fence and looked at Lewis. Then he looked at me. Finally he turned to Hubbard and started talking to him as if they were alone. "I know you think you're doing your duty, following orders. I appreciate that. I was a soldier myself once." He leaned towards us, fingers wound through the iron mesh. "I was in Korea. Men dropped like flies all around me but at least they died in a good cause."

"Back off," Lewis said.

The man went on talking to Hubbard. "Nobody would expect you to stay in there," he said. "All you have to do is walk out and no one will say a thing. If they do I will personally take it up with General Paterson. Word of honor. I'll shake on it." He wiggled the fingers of his right hand.

"Back off," Lewis said again.

The man kept his eyes on Hubbard. He said, "You don't want to stay in there, do you?"

Hubbard looked over at Lewis. A fat bug flew between them with a whine. They both flinched. Then they smiled at each other. I was smiling too.

"You're a smart boy," the man said. "I can see that. Use the brains God gave you. Just put one foot in front of the other."

"You've been told to back off," Hubbard said. "You won't be told again."

"Boys, be reasonable."

Hubbard swung his rifle up and aimed it at the man's head. The motion was natural. The other man leaned out the car window and shouted, "Come on! Hell with 'em!" The deputy chief looked at him and back at us. He took his hands away from the fence. He was shaking all over. A grasshopper flew smack into his cheek and he threw up his arms as if he'd been shot. The car horn honked twice. He turned and walked to the car, got inside, and the two men drove away.

We stood at the fence and watched the car until it disappeared around a curve.

"It's no big deal," I said. "They'll put the fire out."

And so they did. But before that happened there was one bad moment when the wind shifted in our direction. We had our first taste of smoke then. The air was full of insects flying away from the fire, all kinds of insects, so many it looked like rain falling sideways. They rattled against the buildings and pinged into the fence.

Hubbard had a coughing fit. He sat on his helmet and put his head between his knees. Lewis went over to him and started pounding him on the back. Hubbard tried to wave Lewis off, but he kept at it. "A little smoke won't hurt you," Lewis said. Then Lewis began to cough. A few minutes later so did I. We couldn't stop. Whenever I took another breath it got worse. I ached from it, and began to feel dizzy. For the first time that day I was afraid. Then the wind changed again, and the smoke and the bugs went off in another direction. A few minutes later we were laughing.

The black smudge above the trees gradually disappeared. It was gone by the time the first sergeant pulled up to the gate. He only spoke once on the drive home, to ask if we had anything to report. We shook our heads. He gave us a look, but didn't ask again. Night came on as we drove through the woods, headlights jumping ahead of us on the rough road. Tall pines crowded us on both sides. Overhead was a ribbon of dark blue. As we bounced through the potholes I steadied myself with my rifle, feeling like a commando returning from a suicide mission.

The first sergeant let us out at company head-quarters. He said, "Sweet dreams, toads," and went off down the street, gunning the engine and doing racing-shifts on the gears.

We turned in our rifles and lingered outside the orderly room. We didn't want to go away from each other. Without saying so, we believed that we had done something that day, that we were proven men. We weren't, of course, but we thought we were and that was a sweet thing to believe for an hour or two. We had stood our ground together. We knew what we were made of now, and the stuff was good.

We sat on the steps of the orderly room, sometimes talking, mostly just sitting there. Hubbard suddenly threw his hands in the air. In a high voice he said, "Boys, be reasonable," and we all started laughing. I was in the middle. I didn't think about it, I just reached out and put my arms on their shoulders. We were in a state. Every time we stopped laughing one of us would giggle and set it off again. The yellow moon rose above the mess hall. Behind us the poker-wise desk clerk, "Chairborne" we called him, typed steadily away at some roster or report or maybe a letter to the girl he dreamed of—who, if he was lucky, kept a picture of him on her dresser, and looked at it sometimes.

4

The three of us fooled around together for the next couple of days. One night we went to a movie in town, but Lewis spoiled it by talking all the time. You'd think he had never seen a movie before. If an airplane came on the screen he said "Airplane." If someone got hit he said "Ouch!" The next night we went bowling and he spoiled that, too. He had to use his left hand because his right hand was still swollen up, and his ball kept bouncing into the gutter. The people in the next lane thought it was funny, but it got on my nerves.

I was in a bad mood anyway. My mother had

called the day after the Fourth to tell me that my car had been located in Bolinas, California. Two hippies were living in it. They said that Keith had sold it to them but they had no idea where he was now. They'd met him by chance in a crash pad in Berkeley. When my mother said "crash pad" I thought, Good God. I could see the whole thing.

She was beside herself. She said that she was going to quit her job and take a bus to San Francisco. Keith could be in trouble. He could be hungry. He could be sick. For a moment she didn't say anything, and I thought, He could be dead. I'm sure that's what she was thinking, too. I told her to stay home. When Keith got hungry he'd be in touch. There was no point in her wandering around a strange city, she'd never find him that way.

"Someone has to look for him," she said.

"Someone like me, you mean." I hadn't wanted to sound so rough. Before I had a chance to soften my words, though, my mother said, "How far away you are. Nothing reaches you."

We patched it up as well as we could. I told her I'd be getting my orders for Vietnam any day now, and promised to look around for Keith while I was in Oakland waiting to ship out.

On Monday the rest of the company returned to duty. Almost everyone had been drinking all weekend, and looked it. Some of the men had been in fights. The ones who'd gone to the beach had terrible sunburns and were forced to walk stiff-legged because they couldn't bend their knees. As they marched they swayed from side to side like penguins. There were over thirty of them in this condition and when we moved out together it was something to see.

Two days later our company was detailed for crowd control. A group of protesters had camped out on the main entrance to the post, on either side of the road. We were supposed to keep them from moving past the gate.

At first it was friendly enough. The protesters waved and threw us sandwiches which we were forbidden to touch. Some of the women were good-looking in a soulful way and that didn't hurt their cause. The men were something else. They were all decked out in different costumes and seemed pleased with themselves in a way that I found disagreeable. There was one in particular I had my eye on. He was always chanting something, and he was the one who finally rounded everybody up and got them on the road.

They stood there for a while. With their arms joined they sang songs. Then they moved toward us. They stopped just short of the gate and began to talk to us. There was a tired-looking blonde girl across from me and next to her was the fellow I'd been watching. I didn't care for him. He was prettier than the girl, and his long black hair curled up at the ends. He looked like Prince Valiant.

The girl said hello, and told me her first name. "What's yours?" she said.

I didn't answer. We'd been told not to, but I wouldn't have anyway.

Prince Valiant shook his head. "You're not allowed to talk," he said. "Doesn't that strike you as paradoxical? Here you are supposed to be defending freedom and you can't talk."

"Why do you want to kill your brothers?" the girl said.

The man next to me began swearing under his breath.

Prince Valiant smiled at him. "Speak up," he said loudly. "Haven't you ever heard of the First Amendment?"

The girl kept talking to me. "Your brothers and sisters in Vietnam don't want a war," she said. "If you didn't go, there wouldn't be any war."

"Don't be a C.I.A. robot," Prince Valiant said.

"Cocksucker," said the man next to me.

Prince Valiant smiled at him. He looked at me. "I think your friend's got a problem," he said.

I was trembling. I wanted to take my rifle to that smile of his and put it down his gullet. The sun was overhead, baking our helmets. Sweat ran down our faces. Everything got quiet. All along the line I could feel the tautness of something about to break. At that moment the highway patrol pulled up, four cars with lights flashing. The patrolmen got out and started clearing the protesters off the road. There was no resistance. Prince Valiant backed away. "You should get some help with that problem of yours," he said to the man beside me, who stepped forward out of line. The blonde girl looked at us. "Please," she said, "please don't." She was pulling on Prince Valiant's arm. The first sergeant yelled at the man beside me to get back in line. He hesitated. Then he stepped back. Prince Valiant laughed and gave us the finger.

The protesters sang more songs, then broke up. After they left we were relieved by another company. I was still trembling. The other men were upset, too. We got back in time for dinner, but hardly any of us went to the mess hall. Instead we sat around and talked about what had happened, and what would have happened if they'd turned us loose. It was the first time I'd joined in a general conversation. While we were talking, Lewis came in. He'd been on KP that day so he'd missed the excitement. He listened for a while, then asked me in a loud voice if I wanted to go see the Bob Hope movie that was playing in town.

Everyone stopped talking.

I told Lewis no, I wasn't in the mood.

He looked at the other men. He stood there for a moment. Then he shrugged and walked outside again.

The stealing began a few days after the protest. A corporal had his wallet taken from under his pillow. It was found beneath the barracks steps, empty. The corporal swore that he'd had over a hundred dollars in it, which was probably a lie. Nobody in the company owned that much money except the clerk-typist, who regularly cleaned everyone out at marathon poker games in the mess hall.

Nothing like this had ever happened before in our company, not in anyone's memory, and everybody assumed that the thief must be from another unit — maybe even a civilian. Our platoon sergeants told us to keep our eyes open. That was all that was said about it.

The next night a man had his fatigue pants stolen while he slept. The thief balled them up and stuffed them into a trash can in the latrine along with his empty wallet. There was something intimate about this theft. Now we all knew, as these things are known, that the thief was one of us.

After the second theft our first sergeant went through all the barracks and made a speech. He had a vivid red scar that ran from the corner of one eye across his cheek and down under his collar. He had been badly wounded in Vietnam, so badly wounded that the Army was forcing him to take early retirement. He had just a few weeks left to go.

The scar gave weight to everything the first

sergeant said. He spoke with painful slowness and agitation, as if each word was a fish he had to catch with his hands. He said that to his mind an infantry company was like a family, a family without any women in it, but a family. He wanted the thief to think about that, and then ask himself one question: What sort of a man would turn his back on his own kind?

"Think about it," the first sergeant said. Then he went to the barracks next door where through the open window we could hear him saying exactly the same thing.

Because the stealing was something new, and I was new, I felt accused by it. No one said anything, but I felt in my heart that I was suspected. It made me furious. For the first time in my life I was spoiling for a fight, just waiting for someone to say something so I could swing at him and prove my innocence. I noticed that Lewis carried himself the same way—swaggering and glaring at everyone all the time. He looked ridiculous, but I thought I understood. We were all breathing poison in and out. It was a bad time.

Hubbard was different. He seemed to wilt. He walked around with his hands in his pockets and his eyes on the ground, and I could hardly get a word out of him. Later I discovered that it wasn't the stealing that got him down, or the suspicion, but pure grief. His friends Vogel and Kirk had been killed, along with their dates, in a car smashup on the Fourth.

We all had our suspicions. My suspicions lay on a man who had never given me any reason to think badly of him. To me he just looked like a thief. I suppose that someone even suspected Hubbard, miserable as he was. If so, Hubbard got clear of suspicion four days after the second theft.

It happened like this. He had left the mess hall early to take a shower. At some point he apparently looked up and saw someone lift his pants off the hook where he'd hung them. He shouted and whoever it was hauled off and hit him dead on the nose. He hadn't seen the thief's face because of the steam in the shower stall, and the blow knocked him down so he had no chance to give chase. His nose was broken, mashed flat against one cheek.

As soon as the story got around, the barracks emptied out. Everyone wanted to get away from the company that night. So did I. But I wanted to see Hubbard even more, partly out of concern and partly for some need that was not clear to me. So I sat on the orderly room steps and waited for him. Men from another company were playing softball on the parade ground. They yelled insults at each other until it got dark and they quit. Then I heard the smaller sounds, moths rustling against the bare light bulb overhead, frogs croaking, one of the Puerto Rican cooks in the mess hall singing happily to himself in that beautiful language that set him apart from us, and made him a figure of fun.

Hubbard came back from the hospital in a white jeep. He was wearing a shiny metal cast over his nose, held by two strips of tape that went across his face. The first sergeant met him and I waited while they talked. When Hubbard finally turned and started towards the barracks, I came up to him. We walked together without speaking for a moment, then I said, "Who was it?"

"I don't know," he said.

I followed him inside and sat on the next bunk while he took his boots off and stretched out, hands behind his head. He stared up at the ceiling. The cast gleamed dully.

"You really didn't see him?" I asked.

He shook his head.

"Well, I didn't do it," I said. "I swear I didn't." Without thinking about it I put my hand over my heart. I could feel my heart beating.

Hubbard looked at me. His lips were pressed together. He was utterly dejected. I could not imagine him pointing a rifle at someone's head. He looked back up at the ceiling. "Who said you did?" he asked.

"Nobody. I just wanted you to know."

"Fine," he said. "I never thought it was you

anyway." Suddenly he turned his head and looked at me again. It made me uncomfortable.

"Just between us," I said, "who do you think it was?"

He shrugged. "I don't know. I'd like to be alone right now if that's all right with you."

"Whatever you want," I said. "If I can do anything, let me know. That's what friends are for."

At first he didn't answer. Then he said, "That was stupid, what we did out at the ammo dump. You probably think it was some big deal, but if you want to know the truth I almost throw up every time I think of it. We nearly got ourselves killed. Don't you ever think about that?"

"Sure I do."

"About being dead? Do you think about being dead?"

"Not exactly."

"Not exactly," he said. "Boy, you're really something. No wonder you like the Army so much."

I waited for Hubbard to go on, and when he didn't I stood up and looked down at him. His eyes were closed. "I'm sorry about what happened to you," I said. "That's why I came by."

"Thanks," he said, and touched the cast on his nose curiously, as if I had just reminded him of it. "It isn't only this," he said. Then, with his eyes still closed, he told me about his friends getting killed.

It spooked me. It was like a ghost story, the way

Hubbard had talked about them so much on the day it happened. I thought I should say something. "That's tragic," I said, the word used in my family for all deaths, and as soon as it was out of my mouth I regretted it. I didn't know then that it is nearly impossible to talk to other people about their own suffering. Instead of giving up I tried again. "I know how you feel," I said. "I'd feel the same way if I lost my best friends."

"You don't have any," Hubbard said, "not like Vogel and Kirk, anyway." He rolled onto his side so that he was facing away from me. "Nobody that close," he said.

"How do you know?" I said.

"I just know."

I understood that Hubbard wanted me to leave. And I was glad to get away from him. It was too late to go anywhere so I went back to my own building. It was empty. I sat down on my bunk. I thought about what Hubbard had said, that I had nobody close. It got to me, coming from Hubbard, because we should have been close after what we'd been through together, he and Lewis and I.

Anyway, it just wasn't true.

I tried to read, but it took an effort in that big quiet room full of bunks. While I stared at the book I thought of other things. I wondered how I would hold up if I got wounded. I'd only been hurt once before, when I was eight, in a fall from a tree. My leg had been broken and I wasn't very brave about it. For several months everyone knew exactly how uncomfortable I was at any given moment. Keith was following me in those days. After I got out of the cast I walked with a limp, and Keith began to limp, too. It drove me crazy. I used to scream at him. Once I shot him with my B-B gun, trying to make him go away—but he kept limping after me, bawling his eyes out.

The door banged open and two men came in, a little drunk. Though it was still fairly early they turned off all the lights and went to bed. I had no choice but to do the same.

For a long while I lay in the dark with my eyes open. My unhappiness made me angry, and as I became more angry I began to brood about the thief. Who was he? What kind of person would do a thing like that?

5

Lewis shuffles along the road leading out of Fort Bragg, muttering to himself and trying to hitch a ride, but he is so angry that he glares at all the drivers and they pass him up. He's angry because he couldn't talk his friends into going to the pictures with him. Bob Hope is his favorite actor but it's not as much fun going alone. He thinks they owed it to him to come.

When he gets to the bottom of Smoke Bomb Hill someone in a convertible stops for him. The driver of the convertible is a teacher who works at the elementary school on post. He is nervous, shy. Lewis leans over the side of the convertible and asks him something which he can't understand because Lewis's voice is so loud and thick. The teacher just keeps looking straight ahead and gives a little nod.

Lewis gets in. He tells the teacher that a fellow in Lawton had a car like this one and drove it across someone's yard one night and got his head cut off by a metal clothesline. They never did find the head, either. Lewis says he figures one of the dogs on the street got ahold of it and buried it somewhere.

He takes out a package of gum and crams four sticks in his mouth, dropping the wrappers on the floor of the car. He has unwrapped the last stick and is about to put it in his mouth when he remembers his manners and holds the gum out to the teacher. The teacher shakes his head, but Lewis stabs it at him until he takes it. When he starts to chew on it Lewis smiles and nods.

They leave the post and head toward town. The road is lined with drive-in restaurants and used-car lots advertising special deals for servicemen. American flags hang limp above the air-conditioned trailers where terms are struck, and salesmen in white shirts stand around in groups. In the early dusk their shirts seem to glow. The air smells of burgers.

The teacher sneaks a look at Lewis. Lewis says something incomprehensible and the teacher looks away quickly and nods. Lewis turns the radio on full blast and starts punching the buttons. When he doesn't get anything he wants he spins the tuning knob back and forth. Finally he settles on a telephone call-in show. People are calling in their opinions as to whether we should drop an atomic bomb on North Vietnam.

A man says we should, right away. Then a woman gets on the line and says that she believes the average person in North Vietnam is probably a lot like the average person here at home, and that their leaders are the ones making the trouble. She thinks we should be patient, and if that doesn't work then we should figure out a way to just bomb the leaders. Lewis chews up a storm. He watches the radio as if listening with his eyes.

He reminds the teacher of one of his students. It's the unfinished face, the way he stares, his restlessness. He asks Lewis to turn down the radio, and as Lewis reaches for the knob the teacher notices his hand—puffed-up and livid. In the five days since Lewis's brush with the nettles the swelling has hardly gone down at all. The teacher asks Lewis what happened to it.

Lewis holds it up in front of his face and turns it back and forth. Nettles, he says. Hurts like hell, too, and that's no lie.

What did you put on it? the teacher asks.

Nothing, Lewis says.

Nothing?

I'm in the Army, Lewis says.

The teacher is going to say that Lewis should go on sick call, but he decides that they've probably bullied him into thinking there's something wrong with that. His father was an Army officer and he knows how they do things. He feels sorry for Lewis, for being helpless and in the Army and having his hand so hideously swollen. You really should put some calamine lotion on it, he says.

Never heard of it, Lewis says.

It's what you do for nettles, the teacher says. It eases the pain and makes the swelling go down.

I don't know, Lewis says. I just as soon wait and see. Every time you go to the doctor it ends up they stick a needle in you.

You don't have to go to a doctor, the teacher says. You can buy it in a drugstore. Lewis nods and looks off. The teacher can tell that he has no intention of spending his money on calamine lotion. He can almost see that hand throbbing away, getting worse and worse, and the boy doing nothing about it. Everybody uses it, he says. We've always got a bottle around.

The teacher is not inviting Lewis to his home. He just wants him to comprehend that calamine lotion is no big undertaking. But Lewis misunderstands. What the hell, he says, I'll try anything once. Long as I get to the pictures by eight.

The teacher turns to explain. But there's no way to do it without sounding like he's backing out. Just before they reach town he pulls off on a side street bordered with pines. Almost immediately the sound of traffic dies. The nasal voice coming out of the radio seems unbearably loud and stupid. It embarrasses the teacher to belong to a species that can think such things. When he stops the car in front of the house he sits for a moment, letting the silence calm him.

They go in through a redwood gate in the back. Lewis whistles when he sees the pool, a piano-shaped pool designed by the teacher's father, who also designed the house. The house has sliding doors everywhere with rice-paper panels. All the drawers and cabinets have brass handles with Japanese ideograms signifying "Long Life," "Good Luck," "Excellent Health." The teacher's father was stationed in Japan after the war and fell in love with Japanese culture. There's even a rock garden in the front yard.

The house is empty. The teacher's mother is

visiting friends in California. His father died two years ago. The teacher leads Lewis to the living room and tells him to sit down. The chairs are heavy and ornately carved. The arms are dragons and the legs are bearded old men with their arms raised to look like they're holding the seats up. Lewis hesitates, then lowers himself into the smallest chair as if that is the polite thing to do.

The teacher goes to the medicine cabinet and takes out the calamine lotion. He comes back to the living room, shaking the bottle. He gives the bottle to Lewis, but Lewis can't open it because of his bad hand, so the teacher takes it back and twists off the cap. He gives the bottle to Lewis again, then sees that Lewis doesn't know what to do with it. Here, the teacher says. Look. He sits in the chair across from Lewis. He pulls the chair close. He pours some lotion into his palm, then takes Lewis's hand by the wrist and starts to work it in, over the swollen, dimpled knuckles, between the thick fingers. Lewis's hand is unbelievably hot.

Hey! Lewis says. That feels fine. I wish I had some before.

The burning skin drinks up the lotion. The teacher shakes more out, directly onto the back of Lewis's wrist. Lewis leans back and closes his eyes. The room is cool, blue. A cardinal is singing outside, one of three birds the teacher can identify. He rubs the lotion into Lewis's hand, feeling the heat leave little by little, the motions of his own hand circular and rhythmic. After a time he forgets what he is doing. He forgets his stomach which always hurts, he forgets the children he teaches who seem bent on becoming brutes and slatterns, he forgets his hatred of the house and his fear of being anywhere else. He forgets his sense of being absolutely alone.

So does Lewis.

Then the room is silent and gray. The teacher has no idea when the bird stopped singing. He looks down where his hand and Lewis's are joined, fingers interlaced. For once Lewis is still. He breathes so peacefully and deeply that the teacher thinks he is asleep. Then he sees that Lewis's eyes are open. There is a thin gleam of light upon them.

The teacher unclasps his hand from Lewis's hand.

I have to admit that stuff is all right, Lewis says. I might just go and buy me a bottle.

The teacher screws the cap on and holds the bottle out. Here, he says. Keep it. Go on.

Lewis takes it. Thanks, he says.

The teacher stands and stretches. I guess we'd better go, he says. You don't want to miss that movie.

Lewis follows him out of the house. He stops for a moment by the pool, which the teacher walks past as if it isn't there. The moon is full. It looks like a big silver dish floating on the water. Lewis puts his hand in his pocket and jingles the change.

He and the teacher don't talk on the way to town. Lewis leans into the corner, one arm hanging over the car door and the other on top of the seat. He strokes the leather with just that tenderness his dog used to feel. In town the sidewalks are crowded. Recruits with shaved heads, as many as fifteen or twenty in a group, walk from bar to bar, pushing each other and laughing too loudly, the ones in the rear almost running to keep up. They fall silent when they come up to the clusters of prostitutes, but when they are well past they call things over their shoulders. Different groups shout at each other back and forth across the street. The lights are on over the bars, in the tattoo parlors and clothing stores, in the gadget shops that sell German helmets and Vietcong flags, Mexican throwing knives, lighters that look like pistols, exotic condoms, fireworks and dirty books. The lights flash on the hood of the convertible and along the sides of the cars they pass.

The teacher stops in front of the movie theater. He tells Lewis to be sure and use that lotion and Lewis promises he will. They wave to each other as the convertible pulls away.

The previews are just beginning. Lewis buys a jumbo popcorn and a jumbo coke and a Sugar Daddy. He sits down. A giant tarantula towers over a house. From inside a woman looks out and sees the hairy legs and screams. Lewis laughs. That's some spider, he says out loud. The previews end and the first cartoon begins, a Tom and Jerry. Every time the cat runs into a wall or sticks his tail into a light plug Lewis cracks up. Now and then he shouts advice to the mouse. The couple in front of him move across the aisle and down. The next cartoon is a Goofy. Tinkerbell does the credits, flying from one side of the screen to the other, bringing the names out of her sparkling wand.

Tinkerbell, Lewis says. When he hears the word his stomach clenches. He gets up and walks outside. He stands under the marquee for a moment, just breathing, then runs down the sidewalk in the direction the convertible went, pushing people out of his way without regard. He runs three, four, five blocks to where the downtown ends. His eyes burn from the sweat running into them and his shirt is soaked through. He takes the bottle of calamine lotion out of his pocket and throws it into the road. It shatters. I'm no Tinkerbell, he says. He watches the cars go by for a while, balling and unballing his fists, then turns and walks back into Fayetteville to find a girl.

It is too loud, too bright. One of the women on the street smiles at him but he keeps going. He has never paid for it and he's not about to start now. He's never had it free either, but he came really close once at Nag's Head and has almost managed to forget that he failed. He turns off Combat Alley and heads down a side street. The bars give out. It is quiet here. He passes the public library, a red brick building with white pillars and high windows going dark one by one. A woman holds the door as people leave, mostly old folks. Just before she locks up two girls come out, a fat one in toreador pants and another girl in shorts, her legs white as milk. They both light cigarettes and sit on the steps. Lewis walks to the corner and turns back up the street. He stops in front of the girls. This here the library? he says.

It's closed, the fat one says.

Is that a fact, Lewis says, without looking at her. He watches the one in shorts, who is staring at her own feet and doing the French inhale with her cigarette. He can't see her face very well except for her lips, which are so red they seem to be separate from the rest of her. Shoot, Lewis says, I wanted to get this book.

What book? the fat one asks.

Just a book, Lewis says. For college.

The two girls glance at each other. The one in shorts straightens up. She walks down the steps past Lewis and looks up the street, leaning forward and lifting up one of her long legs like a flamingo.

You're from the post, the fat one says.

Here comes Bo, says the one in shorts. Give me another weed.

Both girls light fresh cigarettes. A car pulls up in

front of the library, a '57 Chevy full of boys. The girl in shorts sticks her head in the window. She backs away, holding a beer and laughing. The door opens. She gets in and the car peels off.

The fat girl says, She is so loose, and grinds out the cigarette under her shoe.

The car stops at the end of the block and comes back in reverse, gears screaming. The door opens again and the fat girl gets in and the car pulls away.

Lewis walks the side streets. He meets no girls, but once, passing an apartment building, he looks in a window and sees a pretty blonde woman in nothing but her panties and bra watching television. He is about to rap on the glass when a little boy comes into the room pulling a wooden train behind him and yelling his head off. The train is on its side. Without taking her eyes off the screen the woman puts the train on its wheels.

Lewis heads back to Combat Alley. There are still a couple of women on the street, but he doesn't know how to go up to them, or what they will expect him to say. And there are all these other people walking by. Finally he goes into The Drop Zone, a bar with a picture of a paratrooper painted on the window.

Most of the prostitutes in town are reasonable women. Their reasons are their own and they aren't charitable, but they aren't crazy either. Mainly they want to do something easier than what they were doing before, so they try this for a while until they find out how hard it is. Then they go back to waitressing, or their husbands, or the bottling plant. Sometimes they get caught in the life, though, and there's a time right after they know they're caught when some of them do go crazy.

Lewis picks out the crazy one in a bar filled with reasonable girls.

She is older than the others and not the best looking, and the trouble she's in shows plainly. She hasn't brushed her hair all day and her dark eyes are ringed with circles like bruises. She is sitting by herself at the bar. The ice has melted in her ginger ale, which she pushes back and forth and never picks up. In a few years she will be talking to herself.

Lewis doesn't even look at any of the others. He is going to do something bad and she is the one to do it with. He goes straight to her and sits on the stool next to her. He avoids the bartender's gaze because he is not sure that he has enough money to pay for liquor and women both. *Liquor and women* are the words that come to his mind. He is really going to do it. Tonight, with her. He swivels on his stool and says, You come from around here?

She can't believe her ears. She stares at him and he looks down. His face is in motion, jerking and creasing and knotting. You want something? she says.

Lewis looks at her and looks away.

Well? she says.

No, he says. I mean maybe I do.

Well do you or don't you?

I don't know, he says. I never paid for it before.

Then go beat your meat, she says, and turns her shoulder to him.

The calamine lotion has dried pink on Lewis's hand and is starting to flake off. He picks at it with a fingernail. How much? he says.

She turns on him. Her eyes are raking his face. What are you trying to pull? she says. You trying to get me jugged or something?

All I said—

I know what you said. Jesus Christ. She dips into her shiny white bag and pulls out a cigarette. She glances around, lights it, and blows smoke toward the ceiling. Drop dead, she says.

Lewis doesn't know what he's done wrong, but he will have a woman and this is the woman he will have. Hey, he says, you ever been to Kentucky?

Kentucky, she says to herself. She grabs her purse and gets off the stool and walks out of the bar. Lewis follows her. When they get outside she whips around on him. Damn you, she says. What do you want?

I want to go with you.

She looks up and down the street. People move past them and no one pays them any attention. You don't give a shit, she says. I get jugged it's all the same to you.

You asked me did I want anything, Lewis says. What are you all mad about?

She says, I had enough of you, and turns away down the sidewalk. Lewis follows her. After a while he catches up and they walk side by side. I'll show you a time, Lewis says. That's a guarantee.

She doesn't answer.

Right down the street from where Lewis threw the bottle of calamine there is a motel with separate little bungalows. She stops in front of the last one. Ten dollars, she says.

How about eight?

Damn you, she says.

It's all I got.

She looks at him for a while, then goes up the steps and unlocks the door and backs into the bungalow. Let's have it, she says, and holds out her hand.

But there are only six ones in Lewis's wallet. He had forgotten the popcorn and the coke and the Sugar Daddy. He hands the money to her. That's six, he says. I'll give you the rest on payday.

Drop dead, she says, and starts to close the door.

Lewis says, Hey! He gets his foot in and pushes with his shoulder. Hey, he says, give me my money back. She pushes from the other side. Finally he hits the door with his whole weight and it gives. She backs away from him. He goes after her. Give me my money back, he says. Then he stops. Put that knife away, he says. I just want my six dollars is all.

She doesn't move. She holds the knife as a man would, not raised by her ear but in front of her chest. Her breathing is hoarse but steady, unhurried.

All right, Lewis says. Look here. You keep the six dollars and I'll bring the rest tomorrow. I'll meet you tomorrow, same place. Okay?

I don't care what you do, she says. Just get.

Tomorrow, he says. He backs out. When he's on the steps the door bangs shut and he hears the lock snap.

The next day Lewis steals the first wallet. It is not under a pillow as the owner later claims but lying on his bunk in plain sight. Lewis sees it on his way to lunch and doubles back when everyone is in the mess hall. It holds two one-dollar bills and some change. Lewis takes the money and tosses the wallet under the barracks steps. He is mad the whole time, mad at the corporal for leaving it out like that and for being so stuck on himself and never saying hello, mad at how little money there is, mad at not having any money of his own.

He doesn't think of borrowing a few dollars

from his friends. He has never borrowed anything from anyone. To Lewis there is no difference between borrowing and begging. He even hates to ask questions.

Later, when he hears that the corporal is telling everyone he had a hundred dollars stolen, Lewis gets even madder. That evening at dinner he stares at the corporal openly but the corporal eats without looking up. On his way out of the mess hall Lewis deliberately bumps against the corporal's chair, hard. He stops at the door and looks back. The man is eating ice cream like nothing happened. It burns Lewis up.

It also burns him up the way everybody just automatically figures the wallet was stolen by an outsider. They are so high and mighty they think nobody in the company could ever do a thing like that. *I'm no outsider*, he thinks. He gets so worked up he can't sleep that night.

The next day Lewis is assigned to a detail at the post laundry, humping heavy bags across the washroom. The air swirls with acrid steam. Figures appear and vanish in the mist, never speaking. It is useless to try and talk over the whining and thumping of the big machines, but now and then someone shouts an order at someone else. Lewis takes one short break in the morning but gets so far behind that he never takes another. All day he thinks about the woman in Fayetteville, how she looks, how bad she is. Doing it for money and carrying a knife. He is sure that nobody he knows has ever had a woman pull a knife on him. He thinks of different people and pictures to himself how they would act if they found out. It makes him smile.

When he gets back to the company he takes a shower and lies down for a while to catch his breath. Everyone else is getting ready for dinner, joking around, snapping each other with towels. Lewis watches them. His eyes sting from the fumes he's been working in and he closes them for a moment, just for a rest, and when he opens them again the barracks is dark and filled with sleeping men.

Lewis sits up. He hasn't eaten since breakfast and feels hollow all through. Even his legs seem empty. He remembers the woman in town, but it's too late now and anyway he doesn't have the money to pay her with. He imagines her sitting at the bar, sliding her glass back and forth.

It starts to rain. The drops rattle on the tin roof. A flash of lightning flickers on the walls and the thunder follows a while after, a rumble like shingle turning in a wave, more a feeling than a sound. Lewis gets up and walks between the bunks until he finds a pair of fatigue pants lying on a footlocker. He picks them up and goes to the latrine and takes the money out of the wallet. A five-dollar bill. Then he stuffs the wallet and pants into the trash can and goes back to bed.

He thinks about the woman again. At first he

was sorry that he didn't meet her when he said he would, but now he's glad. It will teach her something. She probably thought she had him and it's best she know right off the kind of man she is dealing with. The kind that will come around when he gets good and ready. If she says anything he will just give a little smile and say, Honey, that's how it is with me. You can take it or leave it.

He wonders what she thinks happened. Maybe she thinks she scared him off with that knife. *That's a good one*, he thinks, him afraid of some old knife like you'd buy at a church sale. Kitchen knife. He remembers it pointed at him with the dim light moving up and down the blade, worn and wavy-edged from too many sharpenings, and it's true that he feels no fear. None at all.

As he dresses in the morning Lewis looks over at the man he stole from. The man is sitting on his bunk and staring at the floor.

The whole company knows about it by breakfast. And this time they know it's not an outsider but one of their own. Lewis can tell. They eat quietly instead of yelling and stealing food from one another, and nobody really looks at anybody else. Except Lewis. He looks at everyone.

That night the first sergeant comes through and makes a speech. It's a lot of crap about how an infantry company is like a family blah blah blah. Lewis makes himself deaf and leaves for town as soon as it's over.

In town Lewis looks for the woman in the same bar. But she isn't there. He tries all the bars. Finally he walks down to the bungalow. The windows are dark. He listens at the door and hears nothing. A TV on a window sill across the street makes laughing noises. He sits and waits.

He waits for two hours and more and then he sees her coming down the sidewalk with the tiniest little man he has ever seen. You could almost say he's a midget. She's walking fast, looking at the ground just in front of her, and when they get close he can hear her muttering and him huffing to keep up. Lewis comes down the steps to meet them. Hey, says the little man, what the heck's going on?

Beat it, Lewis says.

Okay, okay, the little man says, and heads back up the street.

The woman watches him go. She turns to Lewis. Who do you think you are? she says.

Lewis says, I brought you the rest of the money.

She moves up close. I remember you, she says. You get out of my way. Get!

Here's the money, Lewis says, and holds it out to her.

She takes it, looks at it, drops it on the ground and walks past him up the steps. Four dollars, she says. You think I'd go for four dollars? Get yourself a nigger.

Lewis picks it up. I already gave you six, he says. This here is the rest.

You got a receipt? she says, and sticks her key in the lock.

Lewis grabs her arm and squeezes it. She tries to jerk away but he holds on and closes her hand around the money. That makes ten, he says. He lets go of her arm.

She gives him a look and opens the door. He follows her inside. She turns on the overhead light, kicks her shoes across the room, and goes into the bathroom. He can hear her banging around in there as he sits on the bed and takes off his shoes and socks. Then he stands and strips to his underwear.

She comes out naked. She is heavy in the ankles and legs and walks flat-footed, but her breasts are small, girlish. She drops her eyes as she walks toward him and he smiles.

All right, she says, let's have a look. She yanks his underpants to his knees and grabs him between her thumb and forefinger and squints down while she rolls him back and forth. Looks okay, she says, and drops him. You won't do any harm with that little shooter. Come on. She goes to the bed and sits down. Come on, she says again, I got other fish to fry.

Lewis can't move.

Okay, softy, she says, and goes to her knees in front of Lewis.

No, Lewis says.

She ignores him.

No! Lewis says, and pushes her head back.

Christ, she says. Just my luck. A homo.

Lewis hits her. She sprawls back on the floor. They look at each other. She is breathing hard and so is Lewis, who stands with his fists in front of him like a boxer. She touches her forehead where he hit her. There's a white spot. Okay, she says. She gives a little smile and reaches her hand out.

Lewis pulls her up. She leans into him and runs her hands up and down his neck and back and legs, dragging her fingernails. She stands on his feet and pushes her hips against his. Then she rises up on her toes, Lewis nearly crying out from the pain of her weight, and she presses her teeth against his teeth and licks his mouth with her tongue. She kisses his face and whenever he goes to kiss her back she moves her mouth somewhere else, down his throat, his chest, his hips. She puts her arms around his knees and takes him in her mouth and a sound comes out of Lewis like he has never heard another human make. He puts his hands along her cheeks and closes his eyes.

When he is close to finishing he tries to think about something else. He thinks about close-order drill. They are marching in review, the whole company on parade. The files flick past like rows of corn. He looks for a familiar face but finds none. Then they are gone. He opens his eyes and pulls back.

The regular way, he says. In bed.

He wants to hold her. He wants to lie quiet with her a moment, but she straddles him. She lowers herself onto him and digs her fingers into his flanks so that he rises up into her. He tries to move his own way, but she governs him. She puts her mouth on his and bites him. His foot cramps.

Then she rolls over and wraps her legs around his back and slides her finger up inside him. He shouts and bucks to be free. She laughs and tightens around him. She holds her mouth against his ear and presses with her teeth and murmurs things. Lewis can't make out what she's saying. Then she arches and stiffens under him, holding him so tightly he can't move. Her eyes are open halfway. Only the whites show. Lewis feels himself lift and dip as she breathes. She is asleep.

She sleeps for hours. Nothing disturbs her, not the argument in the street, nor Lewis stroking her hair and saying things to her. Then he falls asleep too.

When he wakes, her eyes are open. She is watching him. Hey there, he says. He reaches out and touches her cheek. He says the same words he was saying before he dozed off. I love you, he says.

She pushes his hand away. You garbage, she

says. She slides off the bed and finds her purse where she dropped it on the floor and takes out the knife. He gets up on the other side and stands there with the bed between them.

You talk to me like that, she says. You come here and mock me. You're garbage. I won't be mocked by you, not by you. You're just the same as me.

Let me stay, he says.

Get out of here, she says. Get! Get! Get!

Lewis dresses. I'll come back later, he says. He goes to the door and she follows him part way. I'll be back, he says. I'll bring you money.

She waves the knife. You'll get this, she says.

It's three o'clock in the morning. The last bus to camp left hours ago so Lewis has to make the trip on foot. The only cars on the road are filled with drunks. They yell things as they drive by. Once a bottle goes whistling past him and breaks on the shoulder. Lewis keeps going, feet sliding in his big square shoes. He doesn't even turn his head.

Just outside the base there is a tunnel with a narrow walkway along the side. The beams from the headlights of the cars glance off the white tiles and fill the tunnel with light. Lewis steadies himself on the handrail as he walks. One of the drivers notices him and leans on his horn and then the other drivers honk too, all together. The blare of the horns builds up between the tiles. It goes on in Lewis's head long after he leaves the tunnel.

He gets back to camp just after dawn and lies on his bunk, waiting for reveille. The man in the next bunk whistles as he breathes. Lewis closes his eyes, but he doesn't sleep.

At reveille the men sit up and fumble their boots on, cigarettes dangling, eyes narrowed against the smoke. Lewis thinks that he was wrong about them, that they are an okay bunch of fellows, not really conceited, just careful who they make friends with. He can understand that. You never know with people. He thinks about what good friends they are to each other and how they held the line in Vietnam against all those slopes. He wishes he had gotten to know them better. He wishes he was not this way.

For the next three days he tries to find a wallet to steal. At night, when he is sure that everyone is asleep, he prowls between the bunks and pats the clothes left on footlockers. He skips meals and checks under pillows and mattresses. As the days pass and he finds nothing he gets reckless. Once, during breakfast, he tries to break into a wall locker where he saw a man put his camera, one of those expensive kind you look through the top of, worth something as pawn, but the lock won't give and the metal door booms like thunder every time Lewis hits it with his entrenching tool. He feels dumb but he keeps at it until he can see there's no point.

During dinner on the fourth night he searches through the barracks next to his. There is nothing. On his way back out he passes the latrine and hears the hiss of a shower. He stops at the door. In one of the stalls he sees a red back through the steam, and, just outside, a uniform hanging on a nail. The bulge of the wallet is clear.

Lewis comes in along the wall. The man in the shower is making odd noises and it takes Lewis a moment to realize that he is crying. Lewis slips the pants off the hook and takes out the wallet. He is putting the pants back when the man in the shower turns around. His pink face floats in the mist. Hey! he says. Lewis hits him and the man goes down without a sound.

Outside the barracks Lewis falls in with the first group of men leaving the mess hall. He heads toward the parade ground and when he gets there he climbs to the top bench in the reviewing stands. He looks over in the direction of the company. No one has followed him, but men are drifting into small groups. They know that something has happened.

Lewis rubs his hand. It is still a little swollen and now it hurts like crazy from the punch he threw. He felt strange doing that, surprised and helpless and sad, like a bystander. What else will he watch himself do? He opens and closes his fingers.

There is a breeze. Halyards spank against the metal flagpole as the rope swings out and back.

He sees right away from the military I.D. that the wallet is Hubbard's. Lewis knows that he and Hubbard had a feeling once between them. He doesn't feel it now and can't recall it exactly, but he wishes he had not hit him. If there'd been any choice he'd have chosen not to. He pockets the money, three fives and some change, and looks through the pictures. Hubbard and a man who looks just like him standing in waders with four dead fish on the ground in front of them, one big one and three just legal. Hubbard in a mortarboard hat with a tassel hanging down. A car. Another car. A girl who looks exactly like Hubbard if Hubbard had a pony tail. An old man on a tractor. A white house. A piece of yellow paper folded up.

Lewis unfolds the paper and reads, *Dear Son.* He looks away, then looks back.

Dear Son, I have some very bad news. I don't think there is any way to tell you but just to write what happened. It was three days ago, on the Fourth. Norm and Bobby went down to Monroe to watch the drag races there. They were double-dating with Ginny and Karen Schwartz. From what I understand they and some of the other kids did a little "celebrating" at the track. Tom saw them and said they were not really drunk but you know how your brother is.

Let's just say he isn't very observant. Norm was driving when they left for home.

They don't know for sure what happened but just the other side of Monroe the car went into a skid and hit a truck parked off the road. Norm and Bobby and Ginny were killed right away. Karen died in the hospital that night. She was unconscious the whole time.

Dear, I know I should have called you but I was afraid I wouldn't be able to talk. Tom and I and Julie and even your father have been crying like babies ever since it happened. The whole town has. Everyone you see is just miserable. It is the worst thing to ever happen here.

This is about all I can write. Call collect when you feel up to it. Dear, don't ever forget that each and every person on this earth is a beautiful gift of God. Remember that always and you will never go wrong. Your loving Mother.

Lewis sits in the stands and shakes his head because Hubbard's mother is so wrong. She doesn't know anything. He would like to know what she thinks when she hears what just happened to Hubbard. Hubbard probably won't tell her. But if she knew, and if she knew about the woman in town and all the things Lewis has done, then she would know something real and give different advice.

He throws the wallet into the shadows under the stands. He starts to drop the letter after it but it stays between his fingers and finally he folds it up again and puts it in his pocket. Then he walks out to the road and hitches a ride to town.

She is not in any of the bars. Lewis goes to the bungalow and shakes the door. You in there? he says. The window is dark and he hears nothing, but he feels her on the other side. Open up, he says. He slams his shoulder against the door and the lock gives and he stumbles inside. From the light coming in behind him he can see the dark shapes of her things on the floor. He waits, but nothing moves. He is alone.

Lewis closes the door and without turning on the light walks over to the bed. He sits down. Breathing the bad air in here makes him light-headed. His arms ache from stacking oil drums all day in the motor pool. He's tired. After a time he takes off his shoes and stretches out on the twisted sheets. He knows that he has to keep his eyes open, that he has to be awake when she comes back. Then he knows that he won't be, and that it doesn't matter anyway.

It doesn't matter, he thinks. He starts to drift. The darkness he passes into is not sleep, but something else. *No*, he thinks. He pulls free of it and sits up. He thinks, *I have got to get out of here.*

Lewis can't tie his shoes, his hands are shaking so. With the laces dragging he walks outside and up the sidewalk toward town. He can hear everything, the trucks gearing down on the access road, the buzz of the streetlights, and from somewhere far away a steady, cold, tinkling noise like someone all alone breaking every plate in the house just to hear the sound. Lewis stops and closes his eyes. Dogs bark up and down the street, and as he listens he hears more and more of them. They're pitching in from every side of town. He wonders what they're so mad about, and decides that they're not really mad at all but just putting it on. It's something to do when they're all tied up. He lifts his face to the stars and howls.

The next morning Lewis wakes up feeling like a million dollars. He showers and shaves and puts on a fresh uniform with sharp creases. On his way to the mess hall he stands for a moment by the edge of the parade ground. They've got a bunch of recruits out there crawling on their bellies and lobbing dummy hand grenades at truck tires. Sergeants are walking around screaming at them. Lewis grins.

At breakfast he eats two bowls of oatmeal and half a bowl of strawberry jam. He whistles on his way back to the barracks. Then the first sergeant calls a special formation and everything goes wrong.

Lewis falls in with the rest of the company. He knows what it's about. *Shoot*, he thinks. It doesn't seem fair. He's all ready to make a new start and he wishes that everybody else could do the same. Just wipe the slate clean and begin all over again. There's no point to it, this anger and fuss, the first sergeant walking up and down saying it gives him nerves to know there's a barracks thief in his company. Lewis wishes he could tell him not to worry, that it's all history now.

Then Hubbard goes to the front of the formation and Lewis sees the metal cast on his nose. *Oh Lord*, he thinks, *I didn't do that*. He stares at the cast. There was a man in Lawton who used to wear one just like it because his nose was gone, cut off in a fight when he was young. Underneath was nothing but two holes.

Hubbard follows the first sergeant up and down the ranks. Lewis meets his eyes for a moment and then looks at the cast again. *That hurts*, he thinks. He will make it up to Hubbard. He will be Hubbard's friend, the best friend Hubbard ever had. They'll go bowling together and downtown to the pictures. The next long weekend they'll hitch a ride to Nag's Head and rustle up some of those girls down there. At night they will go down on the beach and have a time. Light a fire and get drunk and laugh. And when they get shipped overseas they will stick together. They'll take care of each other and bring each other back, and afterwards, when they get out of the army, they will be friends forever.

The first sergeant is arguing with someone. Then Lewis sees that the men around him are emptying their pockets into their helmets and unblousing their boots. He does the same and straightens up. Hubbard and the first sergeant are in front of him again and Hubbard bends over the helmet and takes out the letter that Lewis could not let go of, that he's forgotten does not belong to him.

Where's my wallet? Hubbard says.

Lewis looks down.

The first sergeant says, Where is this boy's wallet?

Under the stands, Lewis says. While they wait Lewis looks at the ground. He sees the shadows of the men behind him, sees from the shadows that they are watching him. The first sergeant is saying something.

Look at him, the first sergeant says again. He puts his hand under Lewis's chin and forces it up until Lewis is face to face with Hubbard. Lewis sees that Hubbard isn't really mad after all. It is worse than that. Hubbard is looking at him as if he is something pitiful. Then Lewis knows that it will never be as it could have been with the two of them, nor with anyone else. Nothing will ever be the way it could have been. Whatever happens from now on, it will always be less.

Lewis knows this, but not as a thought. He knows it as a distracted, restless feeling like the feeling you have forgotten something when you are too far from home to go back for it.

The sun is hot on the back of his neck. A drop of sweat slides down between his shoulder blades, then another. They make him shiver. He stares over Hubbard's head, waiting for the next drop. Out on the parade ground the flag whips in a gust, but it makes no noise. Then it droops again. The metal cast glitters. Everything is still.

6

The morning after Hubbard got his nose broken the first sergeant called a special formation. He walked up and down in front of us until the silence became oppressive, and then he kept doing it. There were two spots of color like rouge on his cheeks. The line of his scar was bright red. I couldn't look at him. Instead I kept my eyes on the man in front of me, on the back of his neck, which was pocked with tiny craters. Finally the first sergeant began to talk in a voice that was almost a whisper. It was that soft, but I could hear each word as if he were speaking just to me.

He said that a barracks thief was the lowest thing there was. A barracks thief had turned his back on his own kind. He went on like that.

Then the first sergeant called Hubbard in front of the formation. With the metal cast and the tape across his cheeks, Hubbard's face looked like a mask. The first sergeant said something to him, and the two of them began to walk up and down the ranks, staring every man full in the face. I tasted something sour at the root of my tongue. I wondered how I should look. I wanted to glance around and see the faces of the other men but I was afraid to move my head. I decided to look offended. But not too offended. I didn't want them to think that this was anything important to me.

I composed my face and waited. It seemed to me that I was weaving on my feet, in tiny circles, and I made myself go rigid. All around me I felt the stillness of the other men.

Hubbard walked by first. He barely turned his head, but the first sergeant looked at me. His eyes were dark and thoughtful. Then he moved on, and I slowly let out the breath I'd been holding in. A jet moved across the sky in perfect silence, contrails billowing like plumes. The man next to me sighed deeply.

After they had inspected the company the first sergeant ordered us to take off our helmets and put them between our feet, open end up. Then he told us to empty our pockets into our helmets and leave the pockets hanging out. My squad leader, an old corporal with a purple nose, said "Bullshit!" and put his helmet back on.

He and the first sergeant looked at each other. "Do it," the first sergeant said.

The corporal shook his head. "You don't have the right."

The first sergeant said, "Do it. Now."

"I never saw this before in my whole life," the corporal said, but he took his helmet off and emptied his pockets into it.

"Unblouse your pants," the first sergeant said.

We took our pantlegs out of our boots and let them hang loose. Here and there I heard metal hitting the ground, knives I suppose.

The first sergeant watched us. He had gotten his wounds during an all-night battle near Kontum in which his company had almost been overrun. I think of that and then I think of what he saw when he looked at us, bareheaded, our pockets hanging down like little white flags, open helmets at our feet. A company of beggars. Nothing worth dying for. He was clearly as disappointed as a man can be.

He looked us over. Then he nodded at Hubbard and they started up the ranks again. A work detail from another company crossed the street to our left, singing the cadence, spades and rakes at shoulder arms. As they marched by they fell silent, as if they were passing a funeral. They must have guessed what was happening.

Hubbard looked into each helmet as they walked up the ranks. I had a muscle jumping in my cheek. And then it ended. Hubbard stopped in front of Lewis and bent down and took a piece of paper from his helmet. He unfolded it and looked it over. Then he said, "Where's my wallet?"

Lewis did not answer. He was standing two ranks ahead of me and I could see from the angle of his neck that he was staring at Hubbard's boots.

"Where is this boy's wallet?" the first sergeant said.

"The parade ground," Lewis said. "Under the stands."

The first sergeant sent a man for the wallet. Nobody spoke or moved except Hubbard, who folded the paper again and put it in his pocket. All my veins opened up. I felt the rush of blood behind my eyes. I was innocent.

When the runner came back with the wallet Hubbard looked through it and put it away.

"You stole from this boy," the first sergeant said. "You look at him."

Lewis did not move.

"Look at him," the first sergeant said again. He pushed Lewis's chin up until Lewis was face to face with Hubbard. They stood that way for a time. Then from behind, I could see Lewis's fatigue jacket begin to ripple. He was shaking convulsively. Everyone watched him, those in the front rank half-turned around, those behind leaning out and craning their necks. Lewis gave a soft cry and covered his face with his hands. The sound kept coming through his fingers and he bent over suddenly as if he'd been punched in the belly.

The man behind me said, "Jesus Christ!"

Lewis staggered a little, still bent over, his feet doing a jig to stay under him. He crossed his arms over his chest and howled, leaning down until his head almost touched his knees. The howl ended and he straightened up, his arms still crossed. I could hear him wheezing.

Then he dropped his arms to his sides and arranged his feet and tried to come to attention again. He raised his head until he was looking at Hubbard, who still stood in front of him. Lewis began to make little whimpering noises. He took a step forward and a step back and then he shrieked in Hubbard's face, a haunted-house laugh that went on and on. Finally the first sergeant slapped him across the face — not hard, just a flick of the hand. Lewis went to his knees. He bent over until his forehead was on the ground. He flopped onto his side and drew his knees up almost to his chin and hugged them and rolled back and forth.

The first sergeant said, "Dismissed!"

Nobody moved.

"Dismissed!" he said again, and this time we broke ranks and drifted away, throwing looks back to where Hubbard and the first sergeant stood over Lewis, who hugged his knees and hooted up at them from the packed red earth.

For the rest of that day we did target duty at the rifle range, raising and lowering man-sized silhouettes while a battalion of recruits blazed away. The bullets zipped and whined over the pits where we huddled. By late afternoon it was clear that the targets had won. We boarded the trucks and drove back to the company in silence, swaying together over the bumps, thinking our own thoughts. For the men who'd been in Vietnam the whole thing must have been a little close to home, and it was a discouraging business for those of us who hadn't. It was discouraging for me, anyway, to find I had no taste for the sound of bullets passing over my head. And it gave me pause to see what bad shots those recruits were. After all, they belonged to the same army I belonged to.

Hubbard ate dinner by himself that night at a

table in the rear of the mess hall. Lewis never showed up at all. The rest of us talked about him. We decided that there was no excuse for what he'd done. If the clerk had busted him at poker, or if someone in his family was sick, if he'd been in true need he could have borrowed the money or gone to the company commander. There was a special kitty for things like that. When the mess sergeant's wife disappeared he'd borrowed over a hundred dollars to go home and look for her. The supply sergeant told us this. According to him, the mess sergeant never paid the money back, probably because he hadn't found his wife. Anyway, Lewis wouldn't have died from being broke, not with free clothes, a roof over his head, and three squares a day.

"I don't care what happened," someone said, "you don't turn on your friends."

"Amen," said the man across from me. Almost everyone had something to say that showed how puzzled and angry he was. I kept quiet, but I took what Lewis had done as a personal betrayal. I had myself thoroughly worked up about it.

Not everyone joined in. Several men kept to themselves and ate with their eyes on their food. When they looked up they made a point of not seeing the rest of us, and soon looked down again. They finished their meals and left early. The first sergeant was one of these. As he walked past us a man at my table shouted "Blanket party!" and we all laughed.

"I didn't hear that," the first sergeant said. Maybe he was telling us not to do it, or maybe he was telling us to go ahead. What he said made no difference, because we could all see that he didn't care what happened any more. He was already in retirement. The power he let go passed into us and it was more than we could handle. That night we were loopy on it.

I went looking for Hubbard. A man in his platoon had seen him walking toward the parade ground, and I found him there, sitting in the stands. He nodded when he saw me, but he did not make me welcome. I sat down beside him. It was dusk. A damp, fitful breeze blew into our faces. I smelled rain in it.

"This is where he went through my wallet," Hubbard said. "It was down there." He pointed into the shadows below. "What I can't figure out is why he kept the letter. If he hadn't kept the letter he wouldn't have gotten caught. It doesn't make any sense."

"Well," I said, "Lewis isn't that smart."

"I've been trying to picture it," Hubbard said. "Did you ever play 'Picture It' when you were a kid?"

I shook my head.

"It was a game this teacher of ours used to make us play. We would close our eyes and picture some incident in history, like Washington crossing the Delaware, and describe what we were seeing to the whole class. The point was to see everything as if you were actually there, as if you were one of the people."

We sat there. Hubbard unbuttoned his fatigue jacket.

"I don't know," Hubbard said. "I just can't see Lewis doing it. He's not the type of person that would do it."

"He did it," I said.

"I know," Hubbard said. "I'm saying I can't *see* him do it, that's all. Can you?"

"I'm no good at games. The point is, he stole your wallet and busted your nose."

Hubbard nodded.

"Listen," I said. "There's a blanket party tonight."

"A blanket party?" He looked at me.

For a moment I thought Hubbard must be kidding. Everyone knew what a blanket party was. When you had a shirker or a guy who wouldn't take showers you got together and threw a blanket over his head and beat the bejesus out of him. I had never actually been in on one but I'd heard so much about them that I knew it was only a matter of time. Not every blanket party was the same. Some were rougher than others. I'd heard of people getting beat up for really stupid reasons, like playing classical music on their radios. But this time it was a different situation. We had a barracks thief.

I explained all this to Hubbard.

"Count me out," he· said.

"You don't want to come?"

Hubbard shook his head. A dull point of light moved back and forth across the metal cast on his nose.

"Why not?"

"It's not my style," he said. "I didn't think it was yours, either."

"Look," I said. "Lewis is supposed to be your friend. So what does he do? He steals from you and punches you out and then laughs in your face. Right in front of everyone. Don't you care?"

"I guess I don't."

"Well, I do."

Hubbard didn't answer.

"Jesus," I said. "We were supposed to be friends." I stood up. "Do you know what I think?"

"I don't care what you think," Hubbard said. "You just think what everyone else thinks. Beat it, okay? Leave me alone."

I went back to the company and lay on my bunk until lights-out. The wind picked up even more. Then it began to rain, driving hard against the windows. The walls creaked. Distant voices grew near as the wind gusted, then faded away. There should have been a real storm but it blew over in just a few minutes, leaving the air hot and wet and still.

After the barracks went dark we got up and made our way to the latrine, one by one. For all the tough talk I'd heard at dinner, in the end there were no more than eight or nine of us standing around in T-shirts and shorts. Nobody spoke. We were waiting for something to happen. One man had brought a flashlight. While we waited he goofed around with it, making rabbit silhouettes with his fingers, twirling it like a baton, sticking it in his mouth so that his cheeks turned red, and shining it in our eyes. In its light we all looked the same, like skulls. A man with a cigarette hanging out of his mouth boxed with his own shadow, which went all the way up the wall onto the ceiling so that it seemed to loom over him. He snaked his head from side to side and bounced from one foot to the other as he jabbed upwards. Two other men joined him. Their dog tags jingled and I suddenly thought of home, of my mother's white Persian cat, belled for the sake of birds, jumping onto my bed in the morning with the same sound.

The man with the flashlight stuck it between his legs and did a bump and grind. Then he made a circle on the wall and moved his finger in and out of it. Someone made panting noises and said, "Hurt me! Hurt me!" A tall fellow told a dirty joke but nobody laughed. Then someone else told a joke, even dirtier.

No one laughed at his, either, but he didn't care. He told another joke and then we started talking about various tortures. Someone said that in China there was a bamboo tree that grew a foot a day, and when the Chinese wanted to get something out of a person or just get even with him, they would tie him to a chair with a hole in the bottom and let the tree grow right through his body and out the top of his head. Then they would leave him there as an example.

Somebody said, "I wish we had us one of those trees."

No one made a sound. The flashlight was off and I could see nothing but the red tips of cigarettes trembling in the dark.

"Let's go," someone said.

We went up the stairs and down the aisle between the bunks. The men around us slept in silence. There was no sound but the slap of our bare feet on the floor. When we got to the end of the aisle the man with the flashlight turned it on and played the beam over Lewis's bunk. He was sitting up, watching us. He had taken off his shirt. In the glare his skin was pale and smooth-looking. The beam went up to his face and he stared into it without blinking. I thought that he was looking right at me, though he couldn't have been, not with the flashlight shining in his eyes. His cheeks were wet. His face was in turmoil. It was a face I'd never really seen before, full of humiliation and fear, and I have never stopped seeing it since. It

is the same face I saw on the Vietnamese we inter-
rogated, whose homes we searched and sometimes
burned. It is the face that has become my brother's
face through all the troubles of his life.

Lewis's eyes seemed huge. Unlike an animal's
eyes, they did not glitter or fill with light. His face
was purely human.

He sat without moving. I thought that those
eyes were on me. I was sure that he knew me. When
the blanket went over his head I was too confused to
do anything. I did not join in, but I did not try to
stop it, either. I didn't even leave, as one man did. I
stayed where I was and watched them beat him.

7

Lewis went into the hospital the next morning. He
had a broken rib and cuts on his face. There was an
investigation. That is, the company commander
walked through the barracks with the first sergeant
and asked if anyone knew who'd given Lewis the
beating. No one said anything, and that was the end
of the investigation.

When Lewis got out of the hospital they sent
him home with a dishonorable discharge. Nobody
knew why he had done what he'd done, though of

course there were rumors. None of them made sense to me. They all sounded too familiar — gambling debts, trouble with a woman, a sick relative too poor to pay doctor bills. The subject was discussed for a little while and then forgotten.

The first sergeant's retirement papers came through a month or so later. He had served twenty years but I doubt if he was even forty yet. I saw him the morning he left, loading up his car. He had on two-tone shoes from God knows where, a purple shirt with pockets on the sleeves, and a pair of shiny black pants that squeezed his thighs and were too short for him. I was in the orderly room at the time. The officer of the day stood beside me, looking out the window. "There goes a true soldier," he said. He blew into the cup of coffee he was holding. "It is a sorry thing," he went on, "to see a true soldier go back on civvy street before his time."

The desk clerk looked up at me and shook his head. None of us had much use for this particular officer, a second lieutenant who had just arrived in the company from jump school and went around talking like a character out of a war movie.

But the lieutenant meant what he said, and I thought he was right.

The first sergeant wiped his shoes with a handkerchief. He looked up and down the street, and though he must have seen us at the window he gave no sign. Then he got into his car and drove away.

All this happened years ago, in 1967.

My father worked at Convair in San Diego, went East for a while to Sikorsky, and finally came back to San Diego with a woman he had met during some kind of meditation and nutrition seminar at a summer camp for adults. They had a baby girl a few weeks after my own daughter was born. Now the two of them run a restaurant in La Jolla.

Keith came home while I was in Vietnam. He lived with my mother off and on for twelve years, and when she died he took a room in the apartment building where he works as a security guard. He's had worse jobs. The manager gave him a break on the rent. All the tenants know his name. They chat with him in the lobby when they come in late from parties, and they remember him generously at Christmas. I saw him* dressed up in his uniform once, downtown, where there was no need for him to have it on.

Hubbard and I got our orders for Vietnam at the same time. We had a week's leave, after which we were to report to Oakland for processing. Hubbard didn't show up. Later I heard that he had crossed over to Canada. I never saw him again.

I never saw Lewis again, either, and of course I didn't expect to. In those days I believed what they'd told us about a dishonorable discharge—that it would be the end of you. When I thought of a dis-honorable discharge I thought of a man in clothes too big for him standing outside bus terminals and sleeping in cafeterias, face down on the table.

Now I know better. People get over things worse than that. And Lewis was too testy to be able to take anyone's word for it that he was finished. I imagine he came out of it all right, one way or the other. Sometimes, when I close my eyes, his face floats up to mine like the face in a pool when you bend to drink. Once I pictured him sitting on the steps of a duplex. A black dog lay next to him, head between its paws. The lawn on his side was bald and weedy and cluttered with toys. On the other side of the duplex the lawn was green, well-kept. A sprinkler whirled rapidly, sending out curved spokes of water. Lewis was looking at the rainbow that hung in the mist above the sprinkler. His fingers moved over the dog's smooth head and down its neck, barely touching the fur.

I hope that Lewis did all right. Still, he must remember more often than he'd like to that he was thrown out of the Army for being a thief. It must seem unbelievable that this happened to him, unbelievable and unfair. He didn't set out to become a thief. And Hubbard didn't set out to become a deserter. He may have had good reasons for deserting, perhaps he even had principles that left him no choice. Then again, maybe he was just too discouraged to do anything else; discouraged and unhappy and afraid. Whatever the cause of his desertion, it couldn't have been what he wanted.

I didn't set out to be what I am, either. I'm a conscientious man, a responsible man, maybe even what you'd call a good man — I hope so. But I'm also a careful man, addicted to comfort, with an eye for the safe course. My neighbors appreciate me because they know I will never give my lawn over to the cultivation of marijuana, or send my wife weeping to their doorsteps at three o'clock in the morning, or expect them to be my friends. I am content with my life most of the time. When I look ahead I see more of the same, and I'm grateful. I would never do what we did that day at the ammunition dump, threatening people with rifles, nearly getting ourselves blown to pieces for the hell of it.

But I have moments when I remember that day, and how it felt to be a reckless man with reckless friends. I think of Lewis before he was a thief and Hubbard before he was a deserter. And myself before I was a good neighbor. Three men with rifles. I think of a spark drifting up from that fire, glowing as the breeze pushes it toward the warehouses and the tall dry weeds, and the three crazy paratroopers inside the fence. They'd have heard the blast clear to Fort Bragg. They'd have seen the sky turn yellow and red and felt the earth shake. It would have been something.

ecco

IN THE GARDEN OF THE NORTH AMERICAN MARTYRS

"Wolff's vision is so acute and his talent so refined that none of [the stories] seem sketchy."
—*New York Times Book Review*

"[Wolff's] ironic dialog, misfit heroes, and haphazard events play beautifully off the undercurrent drift of the searching inner mood which wins over in the end."
—*Chicago Tribune Books*

"I have not read a book of stories in years that has given me such a shock of amazement and recognition—and such pleasure."
—Raymond Carver

"Tobias Wolff is a captivating, brilliant writer, one of the best we've got." —Annie Dillard

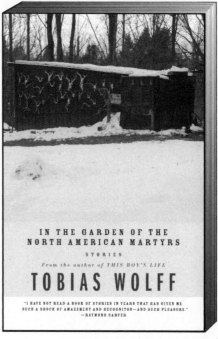

ISBN 0-880-01497-0 (paperback)

A collection of twelve short stories in which Wolff's characters stumble over each other in their baffled—yet resolute—search for the "right path."